For Patty and Jeffrey —MB

For Julia —GP

VIKING
An imprint of Penguin Random House LLC, New York

First published in the United States of America by Viking,
an imprint of Penguin Random House LLC, 2020

LIBRARY OF CONGRESS CATALOGING-IN-PUBLICATION DATA IS AVAILABLE
ISBN 9780593113912

Manufactured in China
Book design by Greg Pizzoli and Jim Hoover Set in Clarion MT Pro

10 9 8 7 6 5 4 3 2 1

JACK AT THE ZOO

Mac Barnett & Greg Pizzoli

1.

THE ZOO

Well, this is the zoo.

The gang is all here.

The gang is the Lady
and Rex and Jack.

The Lady goes
to see the big cats.

Rex barks at the
bats in a dark cave.

Jack sneaks into
cages and tries to
find snacks.

Jack! This cage is not yours.
These are not your snacks.

This guy might share,
but you have to ask.

Jack eats the guy's snacks.
The guy does not fight back.

What's with this guy?
I guess he does not like snacks.

2.

MIX-UP

"Time to close,"
the man from
the zoo says.

The Lady says, “Come, Rex.
Come, Jack! Come back!”

Rex runs up to her.

But where is Jack?

Jack is still in that cage,
with all of those snacks.

The Lady gets help.
"Please help me find Jack.

He has gray fur.
He wears a cap."

Here comes the Lady.
Here comes the man.

Hey! That guy took
the cap off Jack's head.

“There he is,”
says the Lady.

“Yes. There is Jack.”

No! No! But no!

That is not Jack!

3.

NOT JACK

This is not Jack.

He has Jack's cap.
He eats Jack's food and
sleeps in Jack's bed.

He watches TV with
Jack's best friend.

"Jack, you are so good
now," the Lady says.

Not Jack helps
her bake cakes.

Not Jack combs her hair.

Not Jack takes lipstick out of her bag.

"Oh no," says the Lady. "No! Not again! Jack! Don't draw on my walls with that!"

Not Jack helps her
put on makeup.

Then he puts the tube back.

"Wow!" says the Lady.
"You are like a new Jack!"

4.

JACK'S NEW LIFE

Jack sits in a cage
next to three bears.

He waves at the bears.

They glare back at Jack.

At night, the man
from the zoo comes and
drops off some snacks.

The bears grab Jack's snacks
when the man turns his back.

And if Jack tries to cry out,
they reach in and grab Jack.

Jack marks the days
on the floor of his cage.

This is his life now.

A lot of days pass.

5.

NOT JACK'S GOOD DEEDS

Not Jack picks up
trash by the side
of the road.

Not Jack plants
a tree in a ditch.

Not Jack shares a cake
with Rex and some birds.

The Lady stands at the
sink and watches all this.

"You know," says the Lady,
"I think that might not be Jack.
This guy is good.
And Jack tends to be bad."

Will she rush to the zoo?
Will she go get Jack back?

Not Jack comes in and washes the dishes.

The Lady thinks hard.

Then she says,

"Thank you . . . Jack."

6.

JACK'S PLAN

Jack hatches a plan to
escape from his cage.

But Jack needs some help.
He needs help from the bears.

He needs their long arms.
He needs their strong fists.

He draws out his plan.
Hey, that plan looks great!

The bears look at the plan.
The bears look at Jack.
The bears look at each other.

The bears tell on Jack.

The bears sold Jack out!
Hey, bears! What gives?

That night the man gives
the bears extra snacks.

7.

TEATIME

The Lady has tea with
the guy that's not Jack.

She smiles at him.
Not Jack smiles back.

She sips her tea.
Not Jack sips his.

She smiles. He smiles.

They sip and they sit.

The Lady sets
down her teacup.

She says, “I think I miss Jack.”

The Lady goes to the zoo.
She runs and finds Jack.

“There was a
mix-up!” she says.

“That’s Jack there,
in the shirt!”

The man lets Jack
out from the cage.

The Lady hugs him.
Rex licks his face.

Jack gives the Lady
and Rex a big kiss.

It sure is great to have
the gang back!

On their way out, Jack
looks back and feels bad.

Yes, that guy stole Jack's life.
Sure, the bears sold out Jack.

But when Jack looks back,
he still feels bad.

(That's the thing with the zoo.
When you look at the cages,
it can make you feel bad.)

Back at home, the Lady
gives Jack lots of snacks.

“I’m glad you are home,
although you can be bad.

Some bad is good. That’s life.
Some good and some bad.”

When she goes to bed,
Jack picks up her bag.

He takes out her lipstick.

Oh no, Jack! Not that!

Aw, Jack.
That's good.

And that's bad.

The

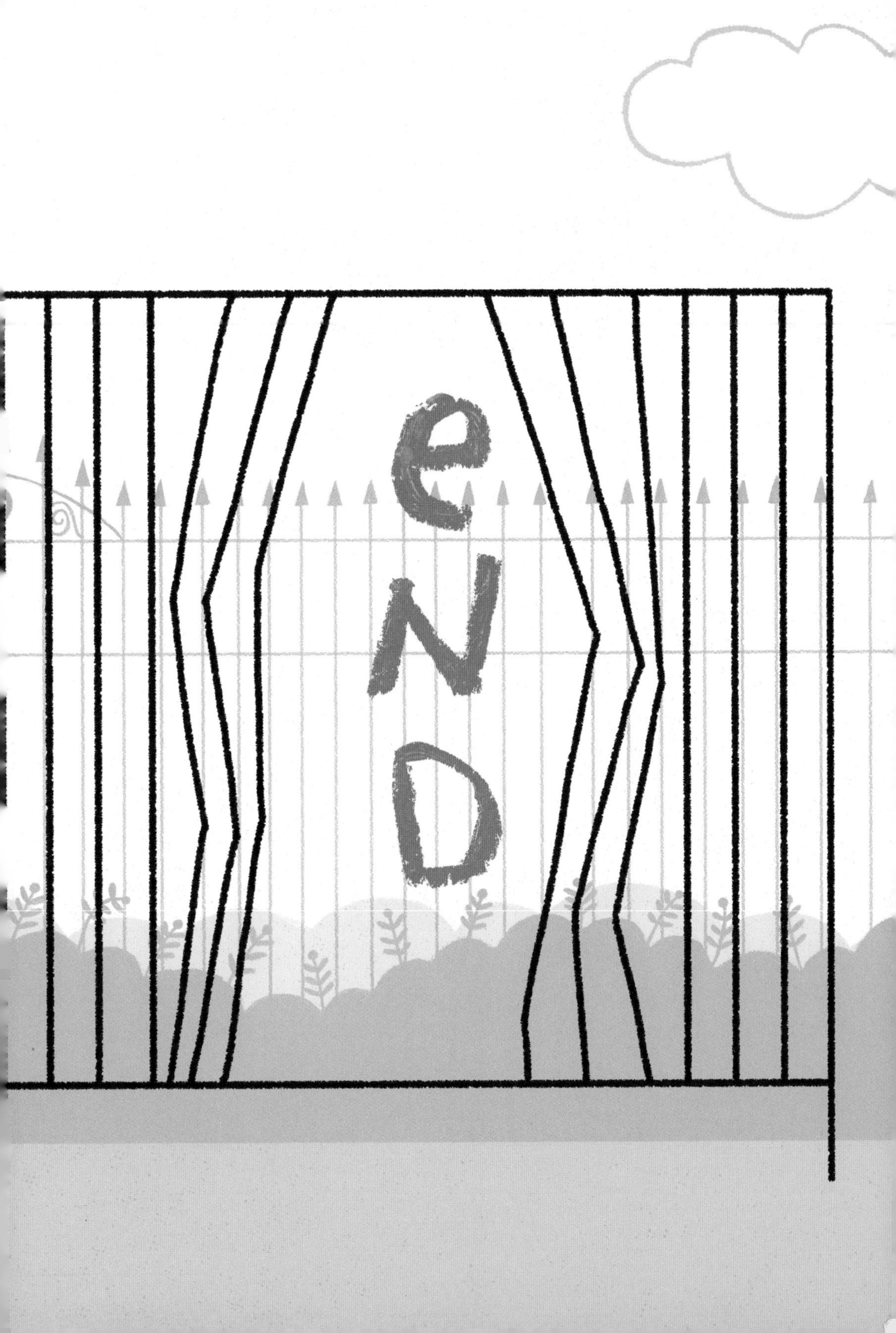
eND

HOW TO DRAW... NOT JACK!

IF YOU WANT MORE JACK, READ:

A JACK BOOK
HI, JACK!
Mac Barnett & Greg Pizzoli

A JACK BOOK
JACK BLASTS OFF!
Mac Barnett & Greg Pizzoli

A JACK BOOK
JACK GOES WEST
$
Mac Barnett & Greg Pizzoli

A JACK BOOK
JACK AT BAT
Mac Barnett & Greg Pizzoli

A JACK BOOK
TOO MANY JACKS
Mac Barnett & Greg Pizzoli